William
1968

HW/Med. Reader

THE PORTABLE MEDIEVAL READER

The Viking Portable Library

Each Portable Library volume is made up of representative works of a favorite modern or classic author, or is a comprehensive anthology on a special subject. The format is designed for compactness and for pleasurable reading. The books average about 700 pages in length. Each is intended to fill a need not hitherto met by any single book. Each is edited by an authority distinguished in his field, who adds a thoroughgoing introductory essay and other helpful material. Most "Portables" are available both in durable cloth and in stiff paper covers.